# AGENT HOPE AND THE LIBERTY DIAMOND

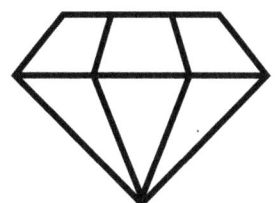

Thanks to

**Tracey Fowler** for allowing the use of photos.

**Tina** whose help made this third book possible.

**Mum** who would have loved the Fowler Herd.

**Donna** for the illustrations.

## Prologue

Throughout the world there are humans who dedicate their lives to care for dogs in wheelchairs and with special needs that most would give up on.

As a thank you to these exceptional people the dogs have created a global organisation to protect the human parents forever more it is called the Defence Global Special Owners or D.O.G.S. for short.

Here is their third story...

# Chapter 1

The sun was warm and bright across the city of Southampton as the D.O.G.S. unit boarded the ship bound for New York.

"Ah Miss Fowler please have some champagne;" a cool glass of fizzy was handed to Tracey, the mum of the now famous Fowler Herd.

"I am Captain Renard, welcome aboard the Queen Mary 2".

Two stewards brought Tracey along a comfortable chair. She sat down and sunk her feet into a bowl of warm water with a big bath bomb bubbling away.

Heath, Merida, Smurfette, Grant, George and Amigo began to lay around the bowl and started to fall asleep.

All except Agent Hope, who decided to follow the captain who was now trying to open some awfully expensive looking luggage.

Unfortunately, the wheels from Hope's cart banged on the metal steps.

The captain turned. "Ahh" he moaned "so many dogs all over my ship!".

He took off his gold braided hat and tried to throw it at Agent Hope who luckily had already got back to the upper deck,

"That was close" Hope thought to herself.

She looked above her and saw a small nose poking out from under a bag of stock from the ship's galley.

"You must be the famous Agent Hope?" came a voice.

" And you are?" demanded Hope.

"I am Special Agent Ziggy, just transferred in from Texas", came the reply.

"Well, are you coming down?" asked Hope.

Ziggy paused "Hold on" his nose scanned the air around them.

Agent Hope looked puzzled "What's up?" she whispered.

Above Agent Hope, the small dog now known as Ziggy, spinned and flipped landing perfectly on his two back wheels.

Unimpressed by Ziggy's actions Hope looked and said, "Very good."

As Ziggy stood in front of her, Hope noticed something not standard issue on the side of her new friend's cart.

Ziggy saw where Hope's eyes were staring.

"Oh yes, that's my sword" Ziggy said proudly.

"When I was a pup, the humans I lived with used to watch a man called Zorro on the TV." Ziggy explained

"He was a great swordsman and I learnt how to use one!".

Ziggy tried to draw his small sword from the side of his cart just as Tracey picked up the little dog, his wheels still spinning.

"Well, everyone" Tracey announced "I hope we would meet up. Please welcome our new member of the Fowler Herd, let me introduce Ziggy!"

## Chapter 2

With her feet getting cold in her bowl, Tracey went to see what all her dogs were doing.

She was met with a view of lots of tails up in the air as all the dogs were looking over the side of their first-class cabin balcony.

They all watched as a large "Silver Ghost" Rolls Royce slowly turned and stopped at the foot of the now red carpeted ramp leading up to the VIP area of the ship.

Agent Heath flipped down his eye scanner and started to focus on the Rolls Royce.

"Okay, Okay, let me zoom in… I've got it!" said Heath.

"And if I try this" He continued pressing a green button, "I should get the local radio station".

Suddenly through the cabin speakers a voice was heard.

"Good morning, you are listening to BBC Radio Solent. Welcome to our show; we believe the Princess is due to arrive at Southampton dockyard anytime now.

"Yes, there's her car, a 1954 Rolls Royce Silver Ghost has just pulled up now".

"Princess Rose has been given the honour of taking the Liberty diamond to New York. It is a gift from Her Majesty the Queen.

Agent Heath said, "I believe it is to go into the torch of the Statue of Liberty

## Chapter 3

The Princess kicked off what she thought were horrible shoes and looked through the large porthole of her VIP cabin.

Two crew members placed her 23 pieces of luggage by the bed.

Using the reflection of the newly polished glass in the porthole, Princess Rose noticed the two crewmen's uniforms were very dirty and they had very hairy hands and dirty fingernails; not like the regular crewmen she was used to.

Thinking the Princess was not looking, the two crewmen tried to take a small black box, the size of a box of chocolates off the bed.

Without turning round, the Princess shouted "You can leave the box where it is, thank you, unless you want Captain Renard to hear about it ".

The crewmen ran out almost falling over each other leaving the box on the bed.

Princess Rose took a key from a gold chain around her neck; opened the box and stared at the diamond sitting on a red velvet cushion, glistening in the light.

The Princess saw the note in gold writing inside the lid.

*"This Liberty diamond is a gift from HRH Queen Elizabeth II and to be placed in the torch of the Statue of Liberty "*

The Princess shut the lid and let out a big sigh.

She heard a lot of noise coming from port side and went to the balcony to see what all the noise was about.

# Chapter 4

A circus was coming aboard.

Clowns, trapeze artists, jugglers and magicians were walking up the gangplank while red, white and blue streamers poured from the upper decks.

The ship's horn sounded as the large propellers started to churn the bluey, green Southampton water.

The Princess looked up into the southern sky. Her eyes spotted something at the very top of the ship's spinning radar dish.

"What is that.... Dog's?" she exclaimed.

# Chapter 5

As their mum was asleep, the agents swung into action.

"Woof, woof... this is Agent Heath come in shepherd unit" he barked

Grant, George, and Amigo were hanging from the radar dish using the super strong ziplines.

Amigo's radio flew out from his headgear. "Heath is that you? He shouted.

Heath replied "How are you getting on with that aerial, we need to talk to homebase"

George hits his radio button with his paw.

"George here, Heath" he called "All okay, aerial fitted, just one problem… Grant's grappling hook has hit this ship's radar dish and is now spinning around …he looks a bit sick".

George looked across to Grant and saw Grant's tail was very firmly between his legs, his ears flat to his head.

"Heath here" Heath called "You will have to get him down before someone sees"

George replied, "we cannot get to him".

Heath thought for a second "Okay"

"Grant, this is Heath" he barked "cut your line and use your parachute".

"Amigo here" radioed Amigo "Grant is shaking his head", "it's OK" replied Heath" I know it's very new but I'm sure I've got it working now"

"Amigo you're going to have to cut his line for him. I have fitted your waistcoat with my next invention… razor sharp cross- bone discs," said Heath.

Amigo, with George holding the lines tight, bent his head and with a loud ting two crossbones spun out from Amigo's waistcoat hitting Grant's line sending the young cadet spinning to the ship's deck below.

## Chapter 6

Agent Heath, confident Grant would be okay, switched off his radio collar and continued exploring the ship.

He found himself in a big dining room with tables all around and humans running about with name tags and fizzy pop of all colours and sandwiches as long as his tail.

There was one table not being looked at.

Heath flipped down his zoom lens over one eye and saw the biggest three-tiered cake he'd ever seen.

He scanned the area and the machine confirmed there were no humans within 20 feet of the target.

"Well," Agent Heath thought to himself "the humans obviously didn't want this cake!".

With the use of his multipaw, Heath got himself up level with the edge of the table. Sliding his wet black nose under the bottom of the cake moved it on the top of his head pushing his ears out flat.

Lowering the robotic legs from his multipaw Heath turned to move very slowly out of the busy room and back onto the open deck of the ship.

Using all his skills, Heath walked very slowly along the deck licking his lips and looking up at his three-tier sponge cake.

Suddenly there was big splodge, and a German shepherd came flying through the cake sending cream everywhere.

"Look out below". came a shout.

It was Cadet Grant on the new parachute Heath had made for him.

Grant barked "it worked" his paws slipping on the cake covered deck.

# Chapter 7

The seventh night of the voyage across the Atlantic was well on its way.

The team of D.O.G.S. agents had now been in touch with Otis and Nordic at homebase who confirmed the mission was to look after the Princess.

Otis reported that he had word from the dockyard D.O.G.S. team and was informed to keep an eye on Captain Renard. With best wishes sent from Chief Nordic the message ended.

## Chapter 8

Passengers walked into the posh dining room. Hats, bow ties and long gowns were the dress code. Each one looking for their name on very large tables full of food ...minus one cake.

Tracey and the herd found their names on cards on the VIP table. She sat down with the herd sitting around her.

And Heath still trying to get the cake out of his ears.

Royal entrance music came from all corners of the room as Princess Rose entered and sat at the top table.

The Princess stood up to start her speech and noticed a dog trying to get cake out of his ears and burst into laughter.

Heath looked up and seemed to give the Princess a big smile.

Smurfette tapped him on his back to let him know the room was waiting.

The Princess began to speak.

"Good afternoon, Ladies and Gentlemen, I've been given the great task of gifting the people of New York and all parts of the USA, the Liberty Diamond ".

Ooohs and Ahhs came from the dining room as the Princess opened the black box sitting on the glass stand in front of her.

The room filled with yellow, blue, and red sparkles with shapes of all sizes.

It's crystal structure bouncing light of the walls and ceiling.

Closing the lid, the Princess continued.

"Her majesty the Queen, has met one of our little friends over there" she said pointing to Tracey and the Herd.

"Her name is Hope".

Hope gave a small curtsey.

"The Queen has requested this special diamond to be created and placed into the torch of the Statue of Liberty and for a powerful light to be put behind it with instructions to wait". She continued;

"Her Majesty hopes that  this is acceptable to the American people ".


Everyone jumped from their seats, applauding and whooping, sending hot dogs and burgers flying from the tables.


"Well, that's nice" Heath said to Hope.

"What the gift" Hope replied as she looked at the box "yes, it is".

"No sorry I meant the hot dogs" said Heath leaping in the air grabbing a flying hotdog "could do with more mustard".


Hope shook her head.

With the room still cheering and applauding, no one noticed the Captain getting to his feet. His fingernails were growing long, digging into the hardwood of the table. Hair started to sprout from his neat white collar. His big smelly claw like feet burst out from his black shiny boots.

Captain Renard: in his anger and rage, accidentally shut off his cloaking device.

Agent Hope's radio sprang into life

"Agent Hope, this is Chief Nordic. Otis has detected the leader of the foxes known as the Man Fox is on the ship with you …".

## Chapter 9

The Man Fox leapt onto the table pulling off the torn Captains' jacket and kicked off his ripped boots. He gave a booming howl to the shocked crowd.

Pushing Princess Rose to the floor he grabbed the black box containing the Liberty diamond.

"Mine all mine" he snarled jumping up and out of the dining room.

All the agents' radios kicked into action.

"This is Chief Nordic; we have a paw red alert! get that box back, all noses to red alert!".

The agent's zoomeeed around the deck of the liner searching for the box as the New York skyline came into view.

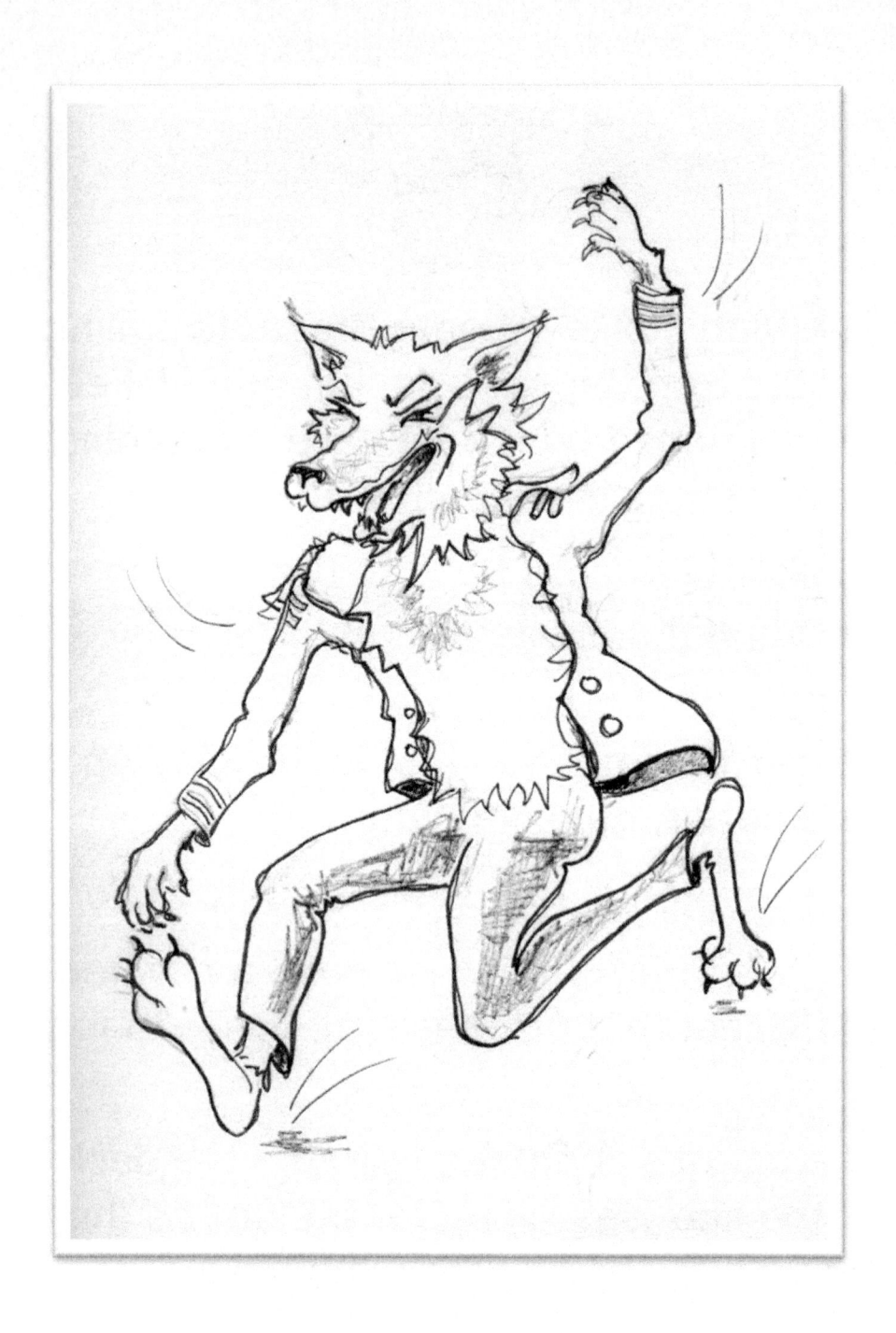

## Chapter 10

A wet black nose hovered over the engine room floor watching massive bits of metal turn and spin. The nose moved up and looked at the crew in the dark engine room.

"Not humans" Agent Hope whispered to herself flipping down her scanner "They're foxes".

Lots of red spots flashed on the scanner, "All Foxes" she confirmed.

Suddenly two blue spots appeared in the corner of the engine room. Agent Hope zoomed in her scanner and focussed on two humans tied up with bags over their heads.

Hope noticed four gold ribbons on the shoulders of the men.

Agent Hope hit a button with her nose the scanner responded… "Four bars are the Captain and Chief Engineer "

"Wow" Hope said, "it's the real Captain".

## Chapter 11

With foxes turning and twisting around the wet and dark engine room, Agent Hope started to slowly sneak across the room getting nearer to the tied-up Captain.

An alarm sounded loudly; it was a trap, but Hope's wheels had already moved too far across the floor.

Zooooooooooooooop

Hope had sprung a rope trap.

As she dangled above them five foxes burst into laughter.

The Man Fox appeared out of the darkness,

"Hello little dog"

Hope was trapped in a cargo net ten feet above the smelly Man Fox.

"You have caused me a lot of trouble with your doggy wood friends "he snarled "I have you now".

Out of nowhere came another voice "You have nothing!"

"What's this another little dog?" exclaimed the Man Fox.

He was right but this was no ordinary dog.

Five Foxes walked in and stood behind the Man Fox welding traditional old boat hooks they had ripped from the wall of the engine room.

"Who are you supposed to be" asked the Man Fox looking down on the dark floor, staring at a small dog with a black mask with little eye holes.

Ziggy remembered back to when he was a pup in Texas watching old episodes of the master swordsman Zorro on an old TV.

He drew the sword from his side with his mouth with the blade catching what little light there was shining back at the Man Fox.

The Man Fox swung the boat hook at Ziggy who darted this way and that spinning on his wheels with his sword deflecting the boat hook each time it came near him.

With the tinging sounds of sword and boathook, Ziggy swished this way and that. He did a full 360 spin and cut the Man fox's boathook in two.

The splintering wood from the hook's handle hit the Man Fox in his face.

Ziggy stopped and looked around the engine room and saw a large pulley. Making sure his wheels were firmly fixed he cut the counterweight and flew up into the air.

Swinging back and forth, he reached out and cut the rope of the cargo net.

Hope fell out of the net and landed in a box of life jackets with a heavy sigh.

"Thank you, Ziggy," Hope said.

"You are free, Senorita" shouted Ziggy in his strong Texan accent as Hope's tail disappeared through the engine room door.

Laughter came from behind Ziggy.

Two foxes joined the fight with long spanners.

More ting ting sounds echoed round the engine room as sparks flew from Ziggy's sword.

Ziggy ran between the two foxes, and they fell together in a heap.

"Ha, having a dance are we little foxes," laughed Ziggy.

The Man Fox tried to do a sneak attack but missed. Ziggy circled the Man Fox and his fox pals tying them up in a knot amongst the engine room machinery.

Seeing an opportunity to copy his hero from the old shows; Ziggy span around on his wheels and saw the ripped trousers of the captain's stolen uniform on the Man Fox and with a swipe of his sword and with great skill, cut through the trousers making a perfect Z on the Man Fox's bum.

# Chapter 12

The Man Fox: holding his rear started ripping out all the engines stop controls, pushing the Queen Mary 2 to full speed as it neared the Brooklyn cruise terminal.

Still holding his bum with one smelly paw and the black box with the Liberty diamond in the other, he headed towards the stern of the great liner leaving his Fox army to hold off Ziggy in the engine room……

With one swish of his sword Ziggy cut the cargo net trapping the pretend engine crew.

Hearing loud howling from the foxes high up in the net; the Man Fox leapt aboard his hidden one-man submarine releasing the docking clamps.

"Ha I'm away" he shouted.

But no, the Man Fox's small submarine did not move.

He looked through his periscope and saw the large anchor chain was jammed in the propellers.

Was it Ziggy? ... No ... was it Hope???

He knew that little dog was strong but this no way ...

A set of grinning teeth showed through the porthole of the sub.

The Man Fox screamed into his radio, calling his fox army.

"This is your boss!" the Man Fox shouted" I order you to come and set me free I'm surrounded by hundreds of German shepherds".

Agent Hope flicked down her eye scope and looked at the Man Fox in his sub.

"A hundred? really?" Hope laughed" because ten is all I see."

It was mighty Agent Tennessee, holding the chain of the sub making sure it could not drop into the sea below.

Hope and Ziggy ran over to the sub and cut the hull door open.

Hope fired her grappling hook which found its mark snatching the black box with the Liberty diamond whipping it back to Hope and securing it to her cart.

Tennessee could not hold the sub anymore.

Ziggy span round hooking the chain to the full net of Foxes and shouted

"Go my smelly friends".

With a whoosh the chain, net and sub shot across the water to where the New York Police were waiting for the now soggy smelly foxes.

Agent Hope's radio kicked in "This is Amigo... we're coming into the terminal real fast!"

## Chapter 13

Ziggy put his sword away and looked up at the smashed controls.

"Amigo... Ziggy here... that Man Fox thing took out everything down here, there's only one way out of this" he called.

"I know" came the reply.

"This is Amigo, calling pursuit agents, Merida and Smurfette. Can you make it to the bridge and stop the ship".

Merida and Smurfette fired their running spikes out of their boots. Two lines of blur zoomed around the passengers so fast the water leapt from the swimming pool as they passed with deck chairs whizzing high up in the air.

Merida and Smurfette blasted onto the bridge of the Queen Mary 2.

"No crew great" Smurfette exclaimed.

"Heath, do you have blueprints for this thing?" asked Merida.

"No Problem, Agents, sending them now" Heath replied.

With blueprints on their scanners, both agents pushed all the buttons they could on the control desk of the bridge.

They finally managed to get to the control jets and pushed hard on every lever as the New York tugboats pushed the liner sideways into harbour.

## Chapter 14

On the dockside, the band started playing the American National anthem and then the British anthem.

Cakes were on tables and flags every which way.

The New York city Mayor walked up to the microphone.

Just as he just opened his mouth to speak, a ten-foot wave knocked the mayor, band and cakes across the harbour.

A soggy mayor looked up and saw the Queen Mary 2 had finally reached New York and was perfectly docked in the harbour

## Chapter 15

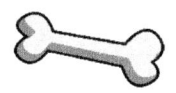

Princess Rose walked tall through a sea of sad faces and picked up the mayor's waterlogged microphone.

"People of New York" she said but the microphone did not work. She looked down at her wet feet and there sitting next to her was a very wet Agent Heath holding a brand-new golden microphone in his mouth.

Taking it, Princess Rose turned it on...

"People" she shouted "Oh it works thank you Doggie" ... "of New York" she continued...

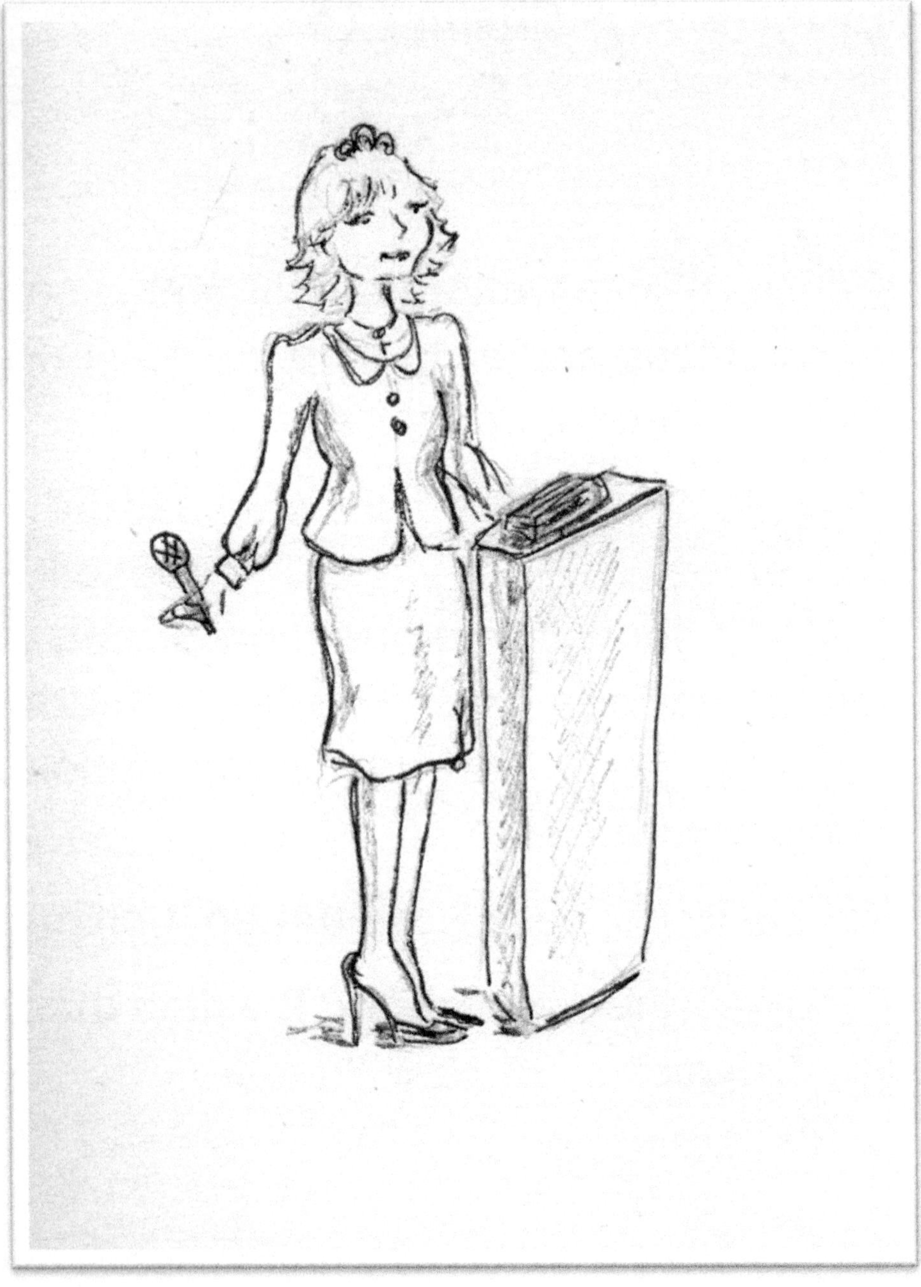

"By the wishes of HRH Queen Elizabeth II, I am to present to you…"

The Princess felt another wet furry dog by her side.

It was Agent Hope with a slightly battered black box still fixed to the top of her cart.

The Princess almost cried as she bent down and hugged the little wet dog.

She jumped up opening the box.

"People of New York" she shouted "from Queen Elizabeth II to you all, I present the Liberty diamond and with the agreement of your president, I would ask you to place this diamond into your great Statue of Liberty's torch and also get the brightest floodlight"

The Princess turned the page of the Queen's instructions "and wait" she said

The crowd went silent and looked at each other with puzzled faces.

No one saw the wet Agent Heath fit in his super candle to the torch which made a super bright light.

Heath's two paws hit the controls and a fantastic light hit the Liberty diamond and a beam shot from the Lady Liberty's torch.

Thousands of triangles and squares flew all around the crowds.

People were there from all over the world, the press, radio, and TV cameras all trying their best to report the scene.

With Heath turning the super candle to full power the squares and triangles began to form dark blob.

All the VIPs and crowd watched.

Princess Rose held Tracey's hand and together with all the Agents, stood watching the blob take shape.

Jaws dropped on all agents faces "Who is that?" asked Princess Rose.

"It's my Nordic" Tracey cried with a proud voice.

# Chapter 16

An image of a massive black German Shepherd was projected from the diamond, his head level with the Statue of Liberty's waist.

"Heath to Otis" Heath whispered, "you have full control of the link from the top of the ship".

A big flash and a zapping sound shot from the ship's radar mast.

Chief Nordic started to bark but then the odd word could be heard.

"My name is Chief Nordic. With Otis tech we have broken the language barrier for a short time. I would like you to remember that like the dogs you see before me, there are dogs like them all over the world.

Some are born needing help and some meet the wrong sort of humans and get hurt.

It is thanks to our mothers, his nose pointed to Tracey; and parents that we do so well.

Remember a word of warning to the humans that would harm us or not be nice to these exceptional humans, the D.O.G.S. organisation is everywhere.

This image will not speak again but will remain as a reminder for the liberty of all animal kind especially the dogs".


The crowd went crazy as fireworks zoomed through the sky even the band had got the sea water out of their instruments and started to play.

# Princess Rose, Tracey and the herd jumped and danced around statue

# Epilogue

The Vermont woods looked big, with the trees swaying to and fro.

"OK you two. can hear me" Otis called out "yes Sir" came the replies.

"Trainees Toto and Gretchen use your crossbones discs on the cardboard wood fox targets".

Three targets flew up and the trainees both fired and missed all three.

Out of the darkness came a real wood fox

"What have we here? two baby agents?" he snarled.

Toto and Gretchen crawled backwards with their tails tucked under as the wood fox came nearer.

Suddenly a beam of light shone behind the two trainees.

The entire Fowler Herd were lined up with every gadget pointing at the wood fox.

They could hear Tracey walking up to join them so put all their gadgets away.

"Have one of you pooped on the trail again?" asked Tracey "come on, let's go home, my feet are killing me"

Back home all the agents ran into their own beds where they can now be just dogs.

Tracey saw Nordic take a look up into the night sky "looks like snow" he barked, gave a shake and went to his comfy bed.

# CHIEF NORDIC

# AGENT HEATH

# AGENT MERIDA

# AGENT SMURFETTE

# AGENT OTIS

# AGENT HOPE

# CADET GRANT

# AGENT GEORGE

# AGENT AMIGO

# SPECIAL AGENT ZIGGY

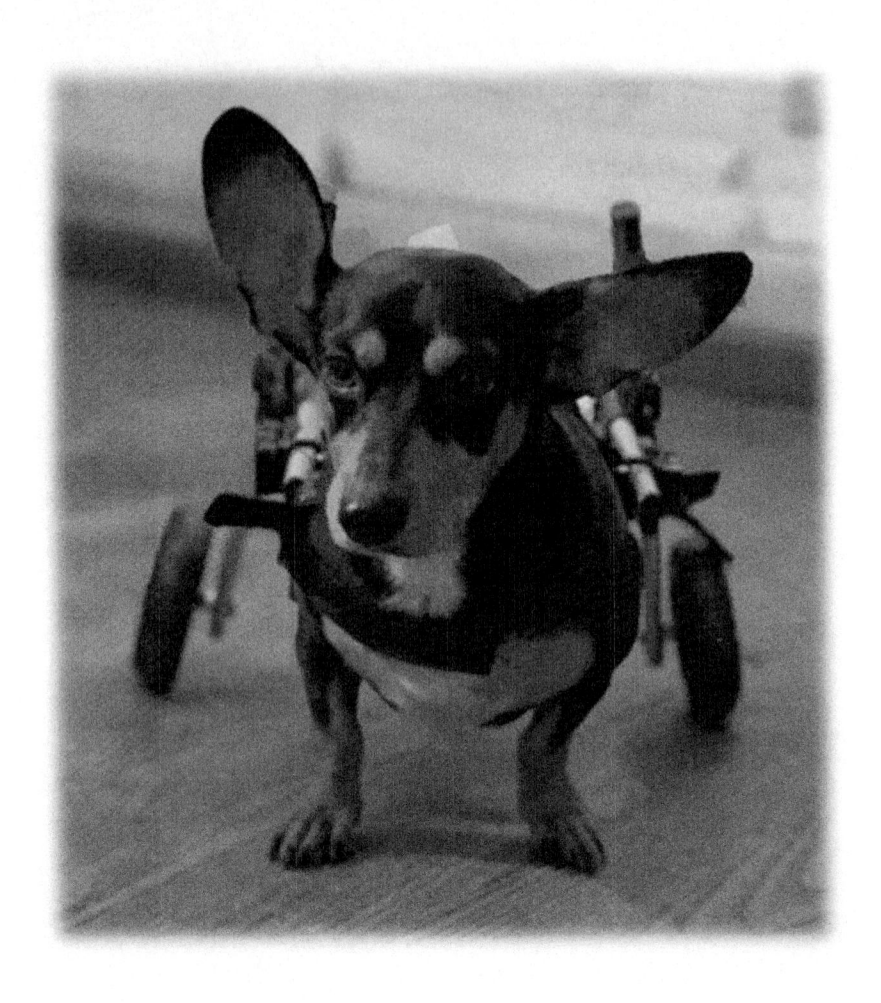

## and introducing
# AGENT TENNESSEE

# TRAINEE GRETCHEN

# TRAINEE TOTO

## Other books in the series by Ian Travers and available on Amazon:

1. Agent Hope and the Wood Fox
2. London Calling Agent Hope

## Useful organisations mentioned by Tracey on her walks:

- ❖ Gunnar's wheels
- ❖ Walking pets by handicapped pets.com

Fowler Herd Merchandise is available from:

www.angelshopeinc.org

www.masonsjourneys.com

www.bonfire.com

www.etsy.com/uk/shop/Knobbalytees

*This book is dedicated to*

*Tracey Fowler*

*An inspirational woman whose love for her herd is unconfined and her posts on Facebook (#The Fowler Herd) brightens everyone's day.*

*And to the three D.O.G.S. agents who are no longer with us*

♥ **Chief Nordic**

♥ **Agent Otis**

♥ **Special Agent Ziggy**

*"Agents stand down and thank you for your service xxx"*

## About the Author:

*Ian with his little girl Quincy – honorary Fowler Herd member and D.O.G.S. UK agent*

Ian Travers has been a follower of The Fowler Herd for several years. Inspired by the dogs and Tracey on her walks he wrote Agent Hope and the wood fox as a gift for her, when Tracey read it she said it had to be printed .... the rest they say is history.

## About the Illustrator:

Donna McGhie is a self employed artist and a level 4 Powertex Fabric Sculpting Tutor.

She is a firm believer in creativity helping with mental health wellbeing. Since 2016 she has been running Art 4 A Heart Powertex workshop to raise money for the Papworth Hospital Charity as a way of saying thank you for saving

her husband's life when he needed an urgent heart transplant.

www.artandmurals.co.uk

Printed in Great Britain
by Amazon